WARNING!

Scaredy Squirrel insists that everyone wash their hands with antibacterial soap before reading this book.

For Francine and Hubert

Published by
HAPPY CAT BOOKS
An imprint of Catnip Publishing Ltd
Islington Business Centre
3-5 Islington High Street
London N1 9LQ

This edition first published 2006
3 5 7 9 10 8 6 4 2

First published in Canada by Kids Can Press Ltd, 29 Birch Avenue,
Toronto, ON M4V 1E2

Text and illustrations copyright © 2006 Melanie Watt
The moral rights of the author/illustrator have been asserted

A CIP catalogue record for this book is available from the British Library

ISBN 10: 1 905117 28 0
ISBN 13: 978-1-905117-28-4

The artwork in this book was rendered in charcoal and acrylic
The text is set in Potato Cut

Printed in Belgium

Scaredy Squirrel

Melanie Watt

HAPPY CAT BOOKS

Scaredy Squirrel never leaves his nut tree.

the unknown

He'd rather stay in his safe and familiar tree than risk venturing out into the unknown. The unknown can be a scary place for a squirrel.

A few things
Scaredy Squirrel
is afraid of:

tarantulas

poison ivy

green Martians

killer bees

germs

sharks

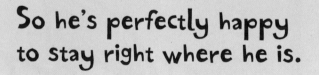

So he's perfectly happy
to stay right where he is.

Advantages of never leaving the nut tree:

- great view

- plenty of nuts

- safe place

- no

Disadvantages of never leaving the nut tree:

- same old view

- same old nuts

- same old place

Monday

Tuesday

Wednesday

Thursday Friday Saturday Sunday

In Scaredy Squirrel's nut tree, every day
is the same. Everything is predictable.
All is under control.

Scaredy Squirrel's daily routine:

6:45 a.m.	wake up	
7:00 a.m.	eat a nut	
7:15 a.m.	look at view	

12:00 noon	eat a nut	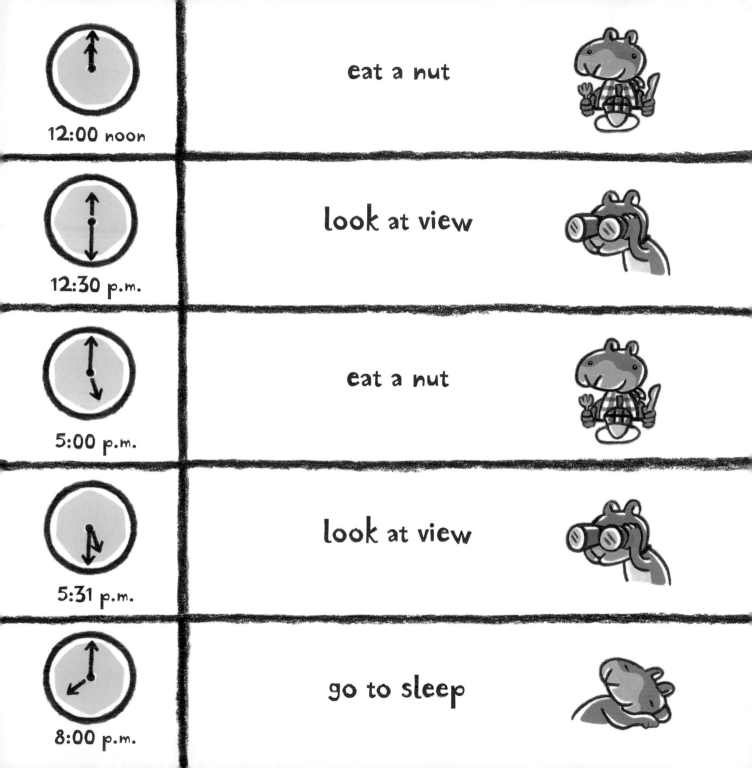
12:30 p.m.	look at view	
5:00 p.m.	eat a nut	
5:31 p.m.	look at view	
8:00 p.m.	go to sleep	

BUT let's say, just for example, that something unexpected **DID** happen . . .

You can rest assured that this squirrel is prepared.

A few items in Scaredy Squirrel's emergency kit:

parachute

bug spray

mask and
rubber gloves

hard hat

antibacterial soap

calamine lotion

net

sticking plaster

sardines

What to do in case of an emergency according to Scaredy Squirrel:

Dramatization

Step 1: Panic

Step 2: Run

Step 3: Get kit

Step 4: Put on kit

Step 5: Consult Exit Plan

Step 6: Exit tree (if there is absolutely, definitely, truly no other option)

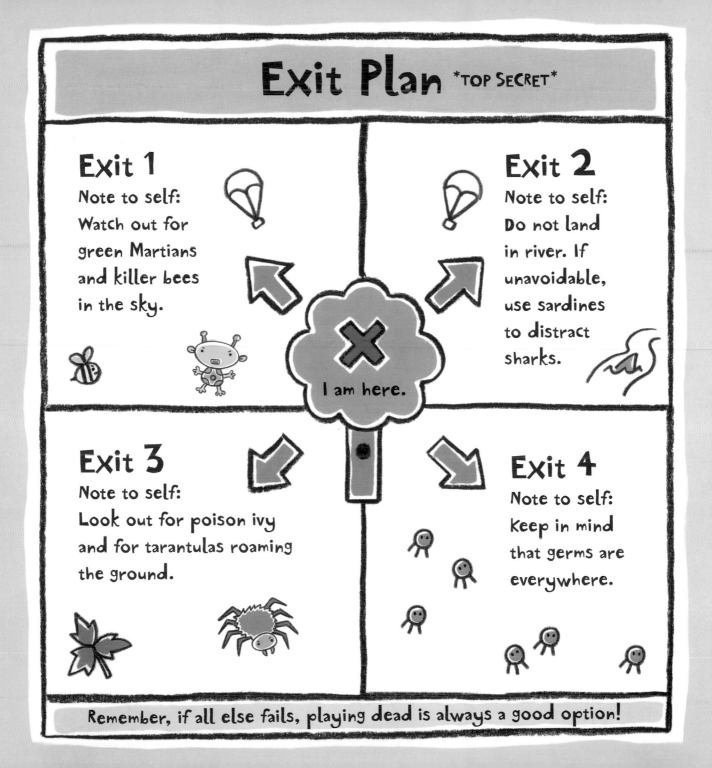

With his emergency kit in hand, Scaredy Squirrel watches. Day after day he watches, until one day . . .

Thursday
9:37 a.m.

A killer bee appears!

Scaredy Squirrel jumps in panic, knocking his emergency kit out of the tree.

This was NOT part of the Plan.

Scaredy Squirrel jumps to catch his kit.
He quickly regrets this idea.
The parachute is in the kit.

But something incredible happens ...

He feels overjoyed!

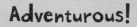

Scaredy Squirrel forgets all about the killer bee, not to mention the tarantulas, poison ivy, green Martians, germs and sharks.

He starts to glide.

Scaredy Squirrel is no ordinary squirrel.
He's a FLYING squirrel!

Finally Scaredy Squirrel realizes that nothing horrible is happening in the unknown today. So he returns to his nut tree.

All this excitement has inspired Scaredy Squirrel to make drastic changes to his life ...

Scaredy Squirrel's new-and-improved daily routine:

6:45 a.m.	wake up	
7:00 a.m.	eat a nut	
7:15 a.m.	look at view	
9:37 a.m.	jump into the unknown	

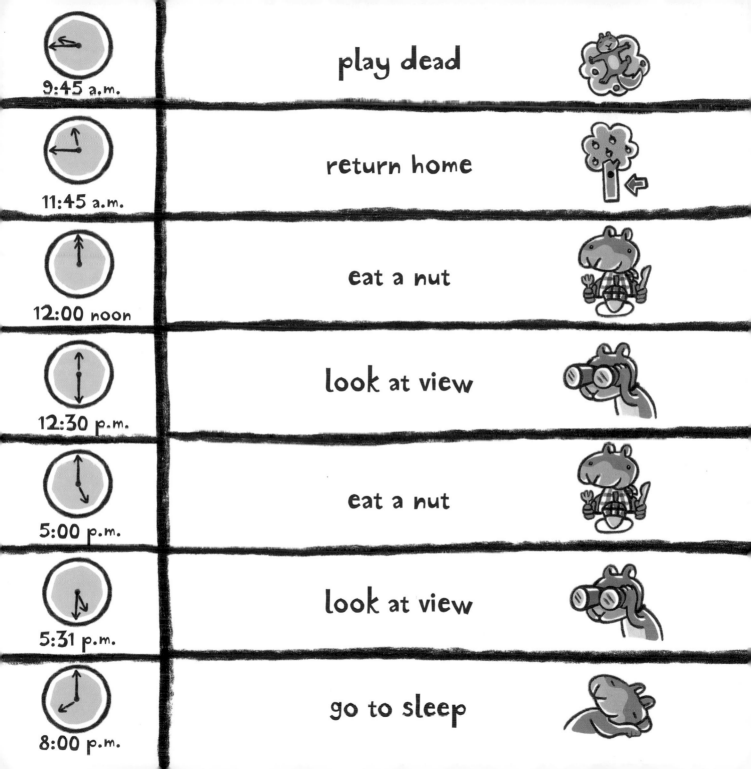

9:45 a.m.	play dead	
11:45 a.m.	return home	
12:00 noon	eat a nut	
12:30 p.m.	look at view	
5:00 p.m.	eat a nut	
5:31 p.m.	look at view	
8:00 p.m.	go to sleep	

poison
ivy

P.S. As for the emergency kit,
Scaredy Squirrel is in no hurry
to pick it up just yet.